Walt Disney's CLASSIC
THE JUNGLE BOOK

Adapted from the Mowgli stories by Rudyard Kipling

A GOLDEN BOOK · NEW YORK
Western Publishing Company, Inc., Racine, Wisconsin 53404

Many strange legends are told of the jungles of far-off India. They speak of Bagheera the black panther and of Baloo the bear. They tell of Kaa the sly python and of the Lord of the Jungle, the great tiger, Shere Khan. But of all the legends, none is so strange as the story of a small boy named Mowgli.

The story began when a child, left all alone in the jungle, was found by Bagheera the panther. He could not give the small, helpless "man-cub" care and nourishment, so Bagheera took him to the den of a wolf family with young cubs of their own.

That is how it happened that Mowgli, as the man-cub came to be called, was raised among the wolves. All the jungle folk were his friends.

Bagheera took Mowgli on long walks and taught him about the jungle.

Baloo the bumbling bear played games with Mowgli and taught him to live a life of ease. There were coconuts for the cracking, bananas for the peeling, and sweet juicy pawpaws to pick from the jungle trees.

Hathi, the proud old leader of the elephant herd, tried to train young Mowgli in military drill as he led his troop trumpeting down the jungle trails.

Sly old Kaa the python would have loved to have squeezed Mowgli tight in his coils. Mowgli's friends warned him against Kaa.

But it was Shere Khan the tiger who was the real danger to Mowgli. That was because Shere Khan, like all tigers, had a hatred of man.

Ten times the rainy season had come to the jungle while Mowgli made his home with the wolf family. Then Shere Khan returned to the wolves' hunting grounds.

The wolf pack met at Council Rock at the next full moon.

"As you know," said Akela, the leader of the pack, "Shere Khan the tiger has returned. If he learns that our pack is sheltering a man-cub, danger will be doubled for all our families. Are we agreed that the man-cub must go?"

Out of the shadows stepped Bagheera the panther.
"I brought the man-cub to the pack," he said. "It is my
duty to see him safely out of the jungle. I know a man-
village not far away where he will be well cared for."

So it was arranged, and when the morning light
slipped through the leaves, Bagheera and Mowgli set out.

All day they walked, and when night fell, they slept
on a high branch of a giant tree. All this seemed like an
adventure to Mowgli, but when he learned that he was
to leave the jungle, he was horrified.

"No!" cried Mowgli. "The jungle is my home. I can
take care of myself. I will stay!"

He slipped down a vine and ran away.

For a while Mowgli joined Baloo, who was bathing in a jungle pool.

Suddenly down swooped the monkey folk, the noisy, foolish *Bandar-log*. They had snatched Mowgli from the pool before Baloo knew what was happening. They tossed him through the air and swung him away through the trees.

Off in the jungle, Bagheera heard Mowgli's cry and came running.

"The monkeys have stolen Mowgli!" gasped Baloo.

Bagheera and Baloo raced off to the ruined city where the monkeys made their home.

They found Mowgli a prisoner of the monkey king.

"Teach me the secret of fire," the monkey king ordered Mowgli. "The magic of fire will frighten even Shere Khan. With it, I shall be the equal of men. Until I know the secret, you are my prisoner."

It took quite a fight for Bagheera and Baloo to rescue Mowgli that time! But the foolish boy just stomped and pouted and ran away again.

This time his wanderings led him to where Shere Khan lay waiting in the high grass, smiling a hungry smile.

When Mowgli caught sight of the tiger, Shere Khan asked, "Well, man-cub, aren't you going to run?"

But Mowgli did not have the wisdom to be afraid. "Why should I run?" he asked, staring Shere Khan in the eye as the tiger gathered himself to spring. "I'm not afraid of you."

"That foolish boy!" growled Bagheera, who had crept close just in time to hear Mowgli.

Both Bagheera and Baloo flung themselves upon the Lord of the Jungle, to save Mowgli once more.

They were brave and strong, but the tiger had razor-sharp teeth and claws.

There was a flash of lightning, and a dead tree nearby caught fire. Mowgli snatched a burning branch and waved it in Shere Khan's face. The tiger, terrified, ran away. Mowgli was very pleased with himself as he strutted between the two weary warriors, Bagheera and Baloo.

Suddenly Mowgli stopped. From ahead came a sound that was strange to him. He peeked through the brush. It was the song of a village girl who had come to fill her water jar.

As he listened to the soft notes of her song, Mowgli felt strange inside. He felt that he must follow her. Mowgli crept up the path to the village, following the girl and her song.

Baloo and Bagheera watched the small figure as long as it could be seen. When Mowgli vanished inside the village gate, Bagheera sighed a deep sigh.

"It is just as it should be, Baloo," he said. "Our Mowgli is safe in the man-village at last. He has finally found his true home."